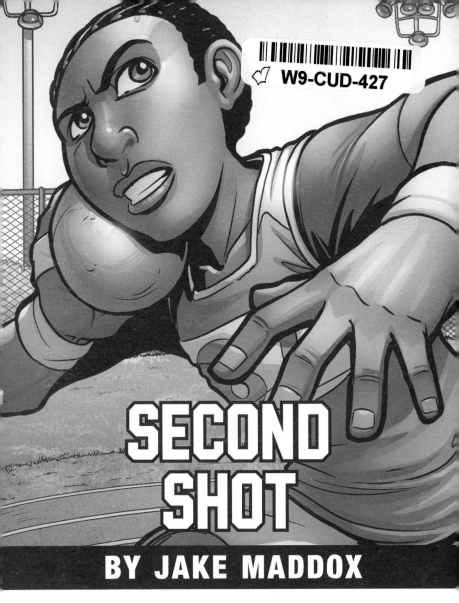

SECOND SHOT

BY JAKE MADDOX

Text by Josh Anderson
Illustrated by Aburtov

STONE ARCH BOOKS
a capstone imprint

Jake Maddox Sports Stories are published by Stone Arch Books
A Capstone Imprint
1710 Roe Crest Drive
North Mankato, Minnesota 56003
www.mycapstone.com

Text and images © 2017 Stone Arch Books

Library of Congress Cataloging-in-Publication Data
Cataloging-in-Publication data is available on the Library of Congress website.
ISBN 978-1-4965-3052-3 (library binding)
ISBN 978-1-4965-3054-7 (pbk.)
ISBN 978-1-4965-3056-1 (eBook (pdf))

Summary: Leggie has always been a natural runner,
but an injury on the first day of practice sidelines him
for the track season. Does he have what it takes to be
a field athlete?

Editor: Gena Chester
Art Director: Russell Griesmer
Graphic Designer: Kyle Grenz
Production Specialist: Gene Bentdahl

Printed in the United States of America.
042016   009736F16

TABLE OF CONTENTS

CHAPTER 1
SERIOUS SHADE... 5

CHAPTER 2
RUNNING INTO TROUBLE 10

CHAPTER 3
OLYMPIC DISAPPOINTMENT 21

CHAPTER 4
A SECOND SHOT.. 26

CHAPTER 4
PUTTING UP NUMBERS 33

CHAPTER 6
SO CLOSE... 40

CHAPTER 7
SHOT DOWN 44

CHAPTER 8
BACK IN THE BLOCKS.. 49

CHAPTER 9
DOWN TO THE WIRE.. 56

CHAPTER 10
A PROMISING FUTURE 61

CHAPTER 1

SERIOUS SHADE

"Woo-hoo! I've got you beat this time, Gary," Leggie said to his friend.

But, when Gary pressed the turbo button on his video game controller his red Ferrari zoomed ahead of Leggie's yellow Lamborghini. "You're too over-confident, man."

Pierce, who'd just started at their school a few weeks before winter break, laughed as Gary's car pulled ahead of Leggie's. "You stink, Leggie. My grandma could beat you."

Leggie frowned, but he was too focused on the race to answer. He wanted to give the new kid a chance, but Pierce seemed more interested in throwing shade than being friends. He was built like a linebacker and had a blond crew cut.

Leggie and Gary had been playing this new racing video game at Gary's house every day after school for the past few weeks, and this was the closest Leggie had gotten to winning. He came to a sharp turn and saw his car heading into the wall on the side of the track. He eased up on the accelerator for a second. Gary, though, handled the turn perfectly and took an even bigger lead.

A few seconds later, Gary's car crossed the finish line.

"You got lucky again!" Leggie said to his friend.

"Yeah, just like you got lucky in Regionals last season," Gary answered. Leggie and Gary were the two fastest guys on the Bricklin Middle School track and field team. They had a friendly competition that carried into every practice, and even every track meet. The two boys always compared their results against each other, even when they were part of the same team in the 1600-meter relay.

Last season, Leggie outran almost everyone he competed against. He planned to pick up right where he left off. The first practice of the season was still two days away, but Leggie wished it was right now. Playing video games was fun and all, but LaGrande "Leggie" Peters felt happiest when he was moving down the track, leaving the competition in the dust.

Leggie was born to run, with a tall, lean frame. Leggie's favorite picture of himself was from a track meet two years ago. Someone else wouldn't even recognize the blur racing past the other runners on his way to winning the race. But Leggie loved the image.

"No one in the state of Illinois is going to stand a chance against our team this year," Leggie said. He jumped up when he looked at the clock on the wall. It was five minutes until dinnertime at his house. "I'm late!" he said. "My mom threatened to ground me if I didn't have the table set by six."

He gave a quick fist bump to Gary, and one to Pierce also.

"Later, mama's boy," Pierce said mockingly. "I hope she's not too mad at her little boo bear."

"Uh . . . later," Leggie said as he bolted down the hall and out of the house. He wasn't sure about Pierce. Gary liked him, but it seemed like the guy's favorite thing to do was make fun of everyone else.

CHAPTER 2

RUNNING INTO TROUBLE

Leggie's running spikes clawed into the track as he warmed up before the first practice of the season. Being on the track again felt amazing. Running had always come easy to Leggie. It wasn't that he didn't train hard. He'd just always been faster than all of the other kids he'd known.

He thought he might feel rusty. It had been months since the last track practice, and the bad weather over the last few weeks had made it hard to get outside and run. But, actually, Leggie felt great.

He moved down the track quickly, and caught up to Gary who was lightly jogging.

"You're not gonna win Regionals running like that," Leggie said, with a laugh, blowing by him, but then slowing down to let Gary catch up. He and Gary looked like they could be brothers, except Leggie was a couple of inches taller. The boys had turned trash talking to each other into an art form.

"You realize it's the first practice of the year, right?" Gary asked with a smile. "Pace yourself. Regionals are still months away."

"Train fast, race fast," Leggie said.

"Train tight, race never," Gary answered. "Don't hurt yourself, man. There's no way we'll lose the 1600-meter relay if we're both out there running."

"Boom!" Leggie said, giving his buddy a fist bump.

Leggie hadn't told Gary about the envelope Coach Crespi had given him before practice. It was from the Waukegan Footprints Track Club, the most prestigious racing club in northern Illinois. Leggie only had a minute to read the letter before stuffing it into his book bag to look at again later. But every time he thought about it his heart started racing.

Leggie pointed at a bunch of their teammates stretching in the middle of the track. "What's Pierce doing here?"

"I told him we needed throwers," Gary said. "Our best shot put and discus thrower from last season moved on to high school.

"Didn't he have to try out, " Leggie asked?

"Nah. Since he did the throwing events at his old school, Coach didn't think it was necessary. There's not many guys who know how to handle a shot put and discus."

"Dude, it doesn't look that hard," Leggie said, laughing.

Leggie was about to tell Gary he didn't really like Pierce when Coach Crespi blew his whistle, calling the team into the middle of the track.

"The name of the game today is *form*, gentlemen," Coach said a few minutes later, lining up the team's four best runners from last year for a practice relay on the Bricklin Middle School track. Xavier Cho was lined up to go first. Billy Pringles, the shortest kid in school, would race second. He was probably the third fastest guy on the team, after Leggie and Gary.

Gary would go third, and Leggie would run last. The 'anchor' leg went to the fastest guy on the team, and until someone took the honor from Leggie, the spot was his.

"I'm not even timing you guys today," Coach Crespi said. "I just want to see how much you remember from last year. Run right, and the speed will come, boys."

The racers spread themselves out in their starting positions. Coach handed Xavier the red baton, then blew his whistle to start the run. Leggie pulled his ankle up behind him, stretching his quads as he waited for the baton to make its way around to him.

Leggie looked at the rest of the team standing in the middle of the track. Pierce was holding a shot put while one of the assistant coaches mimicked the proper form for throwing.

Some of the guys on the team cheered for the guys running, which made Leggie happy. The guys on the Bricklin team were really supportive of each other. Underneath the joking and the trash talk, everyone had each other's back. From what Leggie saw of Pierce, he wasn't sure whether he was going to fit in.

Leggie hooted with the rest of the team as Billy grabbed the baton from Xavier and started jetting up the track. His legs moved faster than anyone else's to make up for his lack of height. It was easy to root for a guy like Billy who, unlike Leggie, had to work twice as hard as anyone else just to keep his spot on the team.

"Look at shrimpy go!" Pierce yelled, loud enough for Leggie to hear over everyone's cheering.

Leggie didn't like it one bit.

Pierce wasn't done with the put-downs. "Mini-me is movin'!" he yelled. Leggie saw a few of the guys standing near Pierce smile at the joke too, which he *really* didn't like. Leggie didn't think it was cool at all to make fun of Billy for his height. It went beyond the kind of trash talk that was fair game on the team.

Leggie was so annoyed and distracted that he lost track of what they were doing. He was staring off into space as Gary raced up behind him and tried handing him the baton for the final leg of the run. Leggie was so startled when he turned around and saw Gary that he fumbled the baton as he grabbed it, and it fell to the ground.

Leggie bent down and reached for the baton as it rolled in front of him.

"Slick grab, Leggie!" he heard someone yell from the sideline. When Leggie eyes shot up for an instant, he saw Pierce laughing and flashed him a quick look.

Finally, Leggie was able to get a hold of the baton and start sprinting down the track. Since he'd messed up the hand-off, he wanted to show Coach that at least his speed was still there.

For a minute, as he ran, Leggie felt the familiar feeling of being "in the zone." His head emptied and all he could hear was the sound of his own breathing. He knew he was making good time as he approached the finish line. *Just a few more yards to go*, Leggie thought, pushing for the finish line. He hoped Coach Crespi would be thrilled to see him already in mid-season form.

Suddenly, Leggie felt a stabbing pain in his right hamstring. He grabbed for the muscle in the back of his leg and hobbled a few more steps before he had no choice but to stop running. He limped over the finish line and sat down on the track. Leggie grimaced as his leg throbbed with pain.

For a minute, Leggie hoped it might just be a cramp. But, when he tried to stand up, he felt the stabbing pain again.

Leggie hit the ground with his hand, the feeling of disappointment almost too much to bear. He couldn't believe he'd gotten hurt on the same day he'd gotten the most important letter of his life.

He put his hands over his eyes so his teammates wouldn't see him, because at the moment there was nothing Leggie could do to stop himself from crying.

CHAPTER 3

OLYMPIC DISAPPOINTMENT

Gary had just come over to drop off Leggie's homework assignments, but Leggie had trouble focusing. He had a huge bag of ice underneath his leg, along with a bunch of pillows elevating it in the air.

Earlier in the day, Dr. Bailey told Leggie he had a grade-two hamstring strain. Leggie couldn't remember any other details except that he wasn't allowed to run for at least eight weeks.

Eight whole weeks, Leggie thought. That meant he'd miss most of the track and field season. At best, he'd be able to return for the last meet of the season, and for the Regional Championship — *if* the team made the Regionals without him. *And even if we do, how am I going to stay in good enough shape to truly compete?*

As Leggie pulled his math notebook from his book bag, he saw the envelope from the Waukegan Footprints Track Club again. He could barely wait for the end of practice yesterday just so he could look at the letter again. But after he hurt himself, Leggie hadn't bothered.

Now, he opened the envelope, and pulled out the letter from Zack Zimmer, a local legend:

Dear LaGrande,

I was impressed with your performance in the 100-, 200-, and 400-meter dashes, and the 1600-meter relay last season. If you can build on your success, I'd like to train you with an eye to the Junior Olympics.

Train hard, eat right, and get plenty of sleep. Let's talk when you have a moment.

Sincerely,

Zack Zimmer

Head Coach, Waukegan Footprints Track Club

Zimmer had sent a lot of local athletes to the Junior Olympics, and even a couple to the Olympic Games.

"How are you feeling, sweetie?" Leggie's mom asked, walking into his room.

Leggie just shrugged. She was the only one who knew about the letter.

"You're gonna heal up in a few months," she said. "Better than ever."

Leggie shrugged again. "Tell that to Zack Zimmer. My big shot is gone, mom. As soon as he hears about the injury, he'll pick someone else to train."

"You caught a bad break, LaGrande," she said. "That's all. You just need to work a little harder to get back to where you were."

Leggie nodded, but he didn't really know what it meant to *work* when it came to track. He'd always just been fast. He trained a lot because it felt good to do something he was so good at.

For the first time in his life, Leggie was dreading track practice.

CHAPTER 4

A SECOND SHOT

Coach Crespi looked over at Leggie, who was hiding out in the stands. "You got some full body injury I don't know about?"

"Huh?" Leggie asked, surprised.

"There's a practice going on," Coach said, "but it looks like you just want to sit on your rear end."

Leggie stood and climbed down from the grandstand, still limping as he moved. He was unsure of what he was supposed to be doing while his teammates practiced.

"It's a miracle! You can walk!" Coach said as Leggie walked up to him. "Listen, LaGrande, I know you're bummed out about your hammy, but how about you try to get something out of practice?"

"Like what?" Leggie asked.

"Hmmm . . ." Coach said, scanning the field. "Go work with Pierce. He's not bad with the shot put."

"Shot put?" Leggie asked. "Really?" He'd never even tried shot put. The 'field' part of 'track and field' always sounded boring to him. The idea of hurling a heavy ball as far as he could just didn't seem all that exciting.

"Better than sitting around," Coach said. "If it hurts your hamstring, you should stop. But at least give it a try."

Leggie nodded, then walked slowly over toward the field. He didn't know which sounded worse, practicing shot put and discus, or practicing them with Pierce.

"Um, Coach said I should work on shot put," Leggie said to Pierce a few moments later. "Because of my leg. I can't run."

Pierce smiled, not even bothering to acknowledge Leggie. Instead, Pierce stuck a *shot* — the heavy ball used in shot put — against the side of his neck, bent his legs, spun and launched the shot down the field.

Leggie was surprised to see Pierce move so gracefully as he spun. He could tell from the look on Pierce's face that his *put* — his throw — had been a good one.

"Nice one," Leggie said, trying again to strike up a conversation.

Pierce snickered and picked up another shot. "Here," he said, tossing it underhand to Leggie.

Leggie bobbled the shot before he caught it. It was heavier than he expected.

"Here goes nothing," Leggie said. He mimicked what he saw Pierce do, sticking the shot against the side of his neck, spinning and pushing the shot into the air ahead of him.

The shot only traveled a few feet, and he heard Pierce laugh.

Leggie's hamstring hurt a little from his first try, but he felt a surge of competitiveness now. He might not be able to outdo Pierce, but he wasn't going to give him any ammunition to call him a 'quitter' either.

Leggie picked up another shot, and tried again. This one hung in the air for much longer before it landed. It was still short of Pierce's attempt, but much closer than Leggie's first try.

"Beginner's luck," Pierce said, hurling another shot down the field. It landed in nearly the same spot as his first throw.

Leggie tried a few more times too, but every one of his throws was shorter than the last.

"You might be able to run all day," Pierce said, "but shot put's an endurance sport too. You can't get better if you don't practice, but you can't practice if your upper body is weak." Pierce squeezed Leggie bicep. "How much can you bench?"

"What?" Leggie asked. "You mean bench press?"

"You just answered my question," Pierce said with a smirk. "Runners might be able to skip the weight room, but a shot putter's gotta be strong."

First Pierce made fun of Billy's height, and now he was calling Leggie weak. And lazy!

Leggie didn't say a word to Pierce for the rest of practice. Instead, he fired off practice throws for the next hour, even though his arm felt like jelly and his distances were laughable. He kept thinking about his second throw, which had been almost as long as Pierce's best throw. If Leggie could do it once, he could do it again.

As much as he hated the idea of taking Pierce's advice, he'd need to get stronger if he was going to get better.

CHAPTER 4

PUTTING UP NUMBERS

Leggie kept his routine over the next month secret from everyone except Gary. Every day at lunchtime, the two boys would meet up in Bricklin Middle School's weight room.

They were finishing their workout on the Thursday before the team's third track-and-field meet of the season when Gary caught Leggie looking at himself in the mirror.

"You look bigger, dude," Gary told Leggie. "For real."

Leggie smiled. He couldn't believe how different his body felt in just a month. His work in the weight room was paying off.

"I *feel* stronger, too," Leggie said. "It just stinks that I can't race on Saturday."

"What about shot put?" Gary asked.

"It's Pierce's spot," Leggie said.

"If you beat him in practice today, it might be *your* spot," Gary said.

Coach Crespi always waited until the Friday before a meet to decide which team members were going to compete in which event. Even though Leggie had been getting better, Pierce was still out-throwing him with the shot put most of the time.

"What are we doing in here every day if you aren't going to think positively?" Gary said. "Go out there and *take* the spot!"

Later that afternoon, Leggie was in the middle of having a great practice. So great that he could tell Pierce was feeling nervous, muttering after every one of his own puts that didn't go very far. Just like he had toward the end of every Thursday practice, Coach walked over to Pierce and Leggie.

"You ready to compete, boys?" Coach asked.

Each of them would get two throws, and the one who threw farthest would get to participate in tomorrow's meet against Central Middle School. Pierce was the team's only discus thrower, so he'd be competing in the meet tomorrow no matter what. For Leggie, though, losing now would mean another competition where all he'd get to do was cheer on his teammates.

Pierce went first and his put was a good one.

"Looks like thirty feet," Coach said. "You put that kind of number up tomorrow, you'll probably win the event."

Leggie felt pessimistic after Pierce's throw. He'd *never* had a thirty-foot put.

His first attempt wasn't even close. Barely twenty feet.

"C'mon LaGrande. Don't make it so easy for him," Coach Crespi said. Leggie saw Pierce getting ready for his second throw with a satisfied smile.

With the pressure off, Pierce's second throw went even farther. "What do you think, Coach? Was that 35 feet?"

Coach nodded and smiled. "Close to it."

Unless Leggie could somehow pull out his best put ever, he'd be sitting on the bench again tomorrow.

He took a deep breath and concentrated on the form he'd been working on with Coach over the last few weeks. Even though he couldn't run for another month, his hamstring barely hurt anymore. He could finally bend his legs on his puts, like Coach had shown him.

Leggie pressed the shot to his neck and started his spin. He focused on his lower body.

He came out of his spin and pushed the shot away from his body. It went up into the air and Leggie knew right away that it was a decent put. But, was it *35 feet decent*?

As it landed, Coach jogged out to judge which shot had traveled further. He held up Leggie's shot.

"Welcome back to competition, Leggie Peters," Coach yelled over to them.

Pierce glared at Leggie. "Unbelievable," he said, as he turned and walked off the field, shaking his head

CHAPTER 6

SO CLOSE

Leggie and Pierce avoided each other most of the morning on Saturday, watching the track events from opposite ends of the Bricklin Middle School bench. But, just before Leggie was scheduled to compete in the shot put, Pierce walked up to him.

"Do this, bro," Pierce said. "I don't like it, but you earned it. Now win this."

Leggie was shocked to hear the encouraging words come out of Pierce's mouth. He smiled at his teammate, but was too tongue-tied to say anything back before heading toward the toe box.

Leggie was matched up against Jim Plemons, a guy who looked like he ate shot puts for breakfast. If he'd seen him elsewhere, Leggie would have thought he was in high school, at least. Or maybe, college.

When the gargantuan eighth grader stepped inside the toe box and threw a 36-footer on his first throw, Leggie knew he might be in trouble.

Leggie's first two throws weren't even close. He looked at Pierce, warming up for the discus and wondered whether he would've fared better. After Plemons' last throw, Leggie had one final chance to beat him.

Leggie stepped into the toe box. Again, he dug down deep with his legs and tried to will the shot past the 35-foot marker.

The shot hung in the air for a while, and then hit the ground. It was so close to Plemons' shot that Leggie wasn't sure if he'd won or lost. He ran excitedly onto the field to get a better look, only for his heart to sink when he saw his shot sitting a foot short of Plemons'.

In a close meet, Central Middle School defeated Bricklin Middle School, and Leggie went home that afternoon knowing that another foot on his attempt would've won his team the entire meet.

CHAPTER 7

SHOT DOWN

Over the next few weeks, Leggie's hamstring continued to heal. Meanwhile, he continued his competition with Pierce for the spot as the team's shot putter.

One week, Leggie would win by a narrow margin. The next week, Pierce would win out. Gradually, the mood between them changed. They started acting like teammates in practice and during track meets. The boys even hung out on the weekend a few times.

The more comfortable Pierce got with everyone on the team, the less he acted like a jerk. Leggie even caught him cheering other teammates on during meets.

The week before Regionals, Leggie excitedly knocked on the door to Coach Crespi's office.

"I had a feeling we'd be talking today," Coach said, as Leggie sat in the chair across from his desk.

"So?" Leggie asked. "I'm back! It's been eight weeks. Can I run my four races in the Regionals this weekend?"

"LaGrande, you haven't run all season," Coach said. "And what about shot put?"

"Pierce can do shot put," Leggie said. "My hamstring's felt good for a few weeks now."

"You've become a good shot putter too," Coach said. "I need your focus there."

Leggie's shoulders fell. "But Coach, I can *win* us the 1600-meter relay. And the other races too. I know I can."

"What about the guys who have been running those events all season?" Coach asked. "Should I tell Xavier his spot in the 1600 is gone now? Should I tell Gary, 'Thanks for getting us to Regionals, but you're benched'?"

Leggie didn't know what to say.

"I'm sorry, LaGrande," Coach Crespi said. "I know you didn't expect it, but you've become a shot putter this season. Next year, you'll be right back in the mix for track events. But I've made my decision."

Leggie left Coach Crespi's office deflated. The shot put had been great when running wasn't an option, but Leggie was a runner first. Zack Zimmer had been watching him! If he *could* run, he felt like he *should* run. Suddenly, the shot put didn't feel like enough to him.

CHAPTER 8

BACK IN THE BLOCKS

Leggie woke up on the morning of the Regional Championship meet with a clearer head than he'd had all week. Regardless of what events he was participating in, he was a competitor. He was determined to put forth his best effort to help his team.

Leggie also knew he'd be going up against the best shot putters in the region. If he didn't enter the meet focused and ready to compete, he wouldn't stand a chance.

Most of his teammates were at the track already when Leggie arrived. He smiled, trying to keep a positive attitude, even though the season hadn't gone the way he expected.

As Leggie walked from teammate to teammate giving them fist bumps and high fives, he noticed that Gary wasn't there. He also noticed Coach Crespi walking around nervously, and talking with the other coaches.

Leggie spotted Zack Zimmer sitting in the grandstand, having a conversation with a couple of the race officials. The Waukegan Footprints were a major sponsor of the Northern Illinois Regional Championships.

Before Leggie could ask anyone where Gary was, Coach walked over to him.

"I've got a problem," Coach said. "Gary's got the flu."

Leggie couldn't believe it. Gary was the best runner on the team this season. Losing him would make it very hard for Bricklin Middle School to have a chance to win Regionals.

Leggie didn't wait for Coach Crespi to ask. "I'm ready to run, Coach."

"If you take Gary's spot in the four track events, though, you can't do shot put," Coach said. "It's a four-event limit today."

Leggie thought about it, but it wasn't really a choice for him.

"Pierce is great, Coach," Leggie said. "He'll lock down the shot put for us."

***

Leggie's best event had always been the 100-meter dash. When he lined up at the starting block, he felt ready to finally pick up where he had left off last season. Originally, he'd hoped to break the state record this year, but if he could just win the race today, he'd be happy.

He'd always taken feeling strong and healthy for granted, but for the first time, Leggie felt thankful that his body had healed enough for him to run. He bent down into position and listened for the starter's pistol.

The bang of the pistol rang out into the air and Leggie got a decent jump out of the block. He churned his legs as hard as he could, trying to move the ground beneath him, like coach always told him.

But as Leggie dug his spikes into the track, he couldn't quite get the explosion he wanted. Three other racers jumped out in front of him. The 100 meters was over before he ever had a chance to catch up.

Unfortunately for Leggie, the 200-meter and 400-meter races went similarly. Leggie was always going to be fast, but today he couldn't quite run fast enough.

Leggie hung his head in disappointment. He'd come in fourth in all three events. He wondered whether Coach might choose someone else to run the anchor position in the 1600-meter relay.

Before that final race, though, Pierce was set to take his turn at shot put. Leggie walked up to his teammate, who was warming up.

Neither of them said a word to each other. The arrogant guy Leggie had met over holiday break just wasn't there anymore. And as disappointed as he felt about his own performance, Leggie wanted Pierce to know he was behind him.

"Do this," Leggie said, giving Pierce a double fist bump. Then, he playfully shoved him in the direction of the toe board.

CHAPTER 9

DOWN TO THE WIRE

Pierce had one terrific throw out of his three attempts — enough to earn second place among the eight participants in the shot put. Now it was up to the relay runners. Leggie's team was in second place overall, with only the 1600-meter race to go. If they won the race, Bricklin Middle School would win the Regional Championship.

Leggie looked down the track at Xavier Cho, bent in the starting block with the seven other first-leg runners. He held the baton tightly as he waited for the signal.

Leggie had given his best effort today, but so far, he hadn't done his best running. He hoped that the three racers before him left his team with a chance to win the race. If they did, Leggie was ready to make his 400-meter portion of the race count.

A race official fired the starter's pistol, and the eight runners were off. At first, the racers were all in a tight pack, but Xavier, and a tall runner from Lincoln Middle School pulled ahead as they got close to the first exchange area.

Xavier made a perfect handoff to Billy Pringles. Over his 400-meter stretch of the track, Billy managed to gain a couple of steps on the second Lincoln runner. By the time he handed off to Ivan Rudesky, Bricklin Middle School and Lincoln Middle School were neck and neck for the lead.

Leggie watched Ivan run toward him, the baton moving back and forth as he pumped his arms. He couldn't wait to get his chance.

Suddenly, Ivan stumbled. His knees nearly scraped the ground as he used his free hand to stop himself from falling completely. As Ivan recovered, the racer from Lincoln Middle School took a big lead.

Leggie watched the Lincoln team's baton transfer as their anchor took off toward the finish line. Ivan gritted his teeth and ran hard for him, but it felt like forever until he finally handed the baton to Leggie.

Leggie grabbed the baton from Ivan, and now Leggie moved as fast as he could. For the first time all day, he ran like he had the wind at his back. He was gaining ground on his opponent, but not fast enough.

As they came to the final stretch of track, Leggie was about ten meters behind. It would take a miracle to win, but Leggie knew all he could focus on was running his best race.

He could see the white finish line, standing out against the red track. He pulled within only a few feet of the Lincoln runner. If he only had another 100 meters, Leggie knew he'd take the race. But, now, with less than 25 meters to go, Leggie didn't know if it was possible . . .

CHAPTER 10

A PROMISING FUTURE

The moments after the 1600-meter relay were a blur to Leggie. The finish was so close that the race officials needed to check the video monitor to determine the winner of the race. Minutes seemed to stretch into hours as Leggie and his teammates waited anxiously for the winner to be announced.

"And the results of the 1600-meter relay are in," said a voice over the PA system. "First place goes to Bricklin Middle School."

Leggie couldn't believe it. Winning the race meant they'd won the Regional Championship.

As he and his teammates jumped around and celebrated, Leggie was overcome with happiness. Regardless of what happened in the State Championship later in the month, winning Regionals was something he'd remember for the rest of his life.

Leggie was about to go find his mom in the grandstand when he felt a tap on his shoulder.

It was Zack Zimmer, coach of the Waukegan Footprints Track Club.

"Hi, I'm —"

"Coach Zimmer," Leggie said. "What are you doing here?

The older man smiled. "You never answered my letter."

Leggie didn't know what to say. "I, uh, just thought with my hamstring and all —"

"Oh, come on kid," Zimmer said. "If I gave up on every promising athlete the first time he or she got a little injury, I'd never get my kids anywhere near the Junior Olympics."

"You really think I have a shot?" Leggie asked.

Zimmer smiled at him. "I can't promise anything, but very few athletes who achieve success do it without some bumps in the road. Great track times are only part of the story. You need to be able to ride out the bumps, and you showed this season that you could."

Leggie looked across the field at his teammates. He couldn't wait to share the news with them, especially Gary, and Leggie's new buddy, Pierce.

Then he looked back at Zack Zimmer and smiled. Of course the legendary coach couldn't make any promises. But Leggie felt like his dreams were suddenly within his grasp.

AUTHOR BIO

Josh Anderson is the author of several sports-themed books for kids. He lives and works in the Los Angeles area with his wife, Corey, and their two big guys, Leo and Dane.

ILLUSTRATOR BIO

Aburtov works as a colorist for Marvel, DC, IDW, and Dark Horse and as an illustrator for Stone Arch Books. He lives in Monterrey, Mexico, with his lovely wife, Alba, and his crazy children, Ilka, Mila, and Aleph.

GLOSSARY

anchor (ANG-kur)—the final, and usually fastest, runner in a relay race

baton (buh-TAHN)—a short, thin stick

competition (kahm-puh-TIH-shuhn)—a contest of some kind

concentrate (KAHN-suhn-trayt)—to focus your thoughts and attention on something

endurance (en-DUR-enss)—the ability to keep doing an activity for long periods of time

gargantuan (gar-GAN-chu-uhn)—enormous

hamstring (HAM-string)—a muscle in the thigh that helps to flex and extend the leg

mimic (MIM-ik)—to imitate the actions of someone or something

pessimistic (pess-uh-MISS-tik)—to be gloomy or always think that the worst will happen

pressure (PRESH-ur)—a burden or a strain

prestigious (pre-STEE-juss)—having a high reputation

relay (REE-lay)—a team track event; each team usually has four members

DISCUSSION QUESTIONS

1. Why do you think Pierce makes fun of Leggie and other teammates at the beginning of the story? Talk about some possible reasons he acted the way he did and why he changed later in the story.

2. Gary warns Leggie not to push too hard during the first practice of the season. Leggie doesn't listen and ends up hurting himself. Think of a time you tried too hard, and things didn't work out the way you had planned. Why do you think that happened?

3. Why does Coach Crespi decide to keep Leggie in shot put even though his injury has healed? Discuss whether you agree or disagree with this decision, and explain why.

WRITING PROMPTS

1. Gary helps Leggie with weight training to improve his upper body strength and get ready to compete in shot put. Write about a time a friend helped you prepare for something.

2. At first, Leggie is determined to beat Pierce for the chance to compete at shot put. By the end of the story, he is willing to give his spot at Regionals to Pierce. Write about a time when a rivalry you had turned into a friendship.

3. Coach Zimmer tells Leggie that being able to overcome setbacks is as important as performing well in competitions. Write about a time when you overcame an obstacle, and describe how it made you better.

MORE ABOUT SHOT PUT

People have competed at throwing heavy round stones and cannon balls for centuries. The first appearance of modern shot put dates back to the 19th century Highland Games in Scotland. In these games, competitors threw a round stone or piece of metal from behind a line.

Men's shot put has been an event in the modern Summer Olympic Games since 1896. Women's shot put became an Olympic event in 1948.

The shot, or metal ball, used in shot put is usually made of iron, steel, or brass. The men's shot weighs 16 pounds (7.3 kilograms). Women use a shot that weighs almost 9 pounds (4 kg).

Shot putters make their throws from a 7-foot- (2.1-meter-) diameter circle. For a throw to count, the shot putter cannot step outside the circle or touch the top of the toe-board at the front of the circle.

American shot putter Parry O'Brien invented the glide technique for the sport in 1951. The glide begins with the shot putter facing away from the direction the shot will be thrown. The putter then rotates 180 degrees across the circle before tossing the shot.

In the early 1970s, Soviet shot putter Aleksandr Baryshnikov used a new technique invented by his coach Viktor Alexeyev. Called the spin, it also begins with the putter facing backward. From this position, the putter spins on the ball of the left foot and rotates like a discus thrower. The spinning motion adds power to the throw.

American Randy Barnes set the world record for men's shot put in 1990. He threw a distance of 75.9 feet (23.1 m). Natalya Lisovskaya of USSR set the women's world record in 1987 with a throw of 74.2 feet (22.6 m).